S0-DZL-633

Travel America's Landmarks

Exploring the San Antonio River Walk

by Emma Huddleston

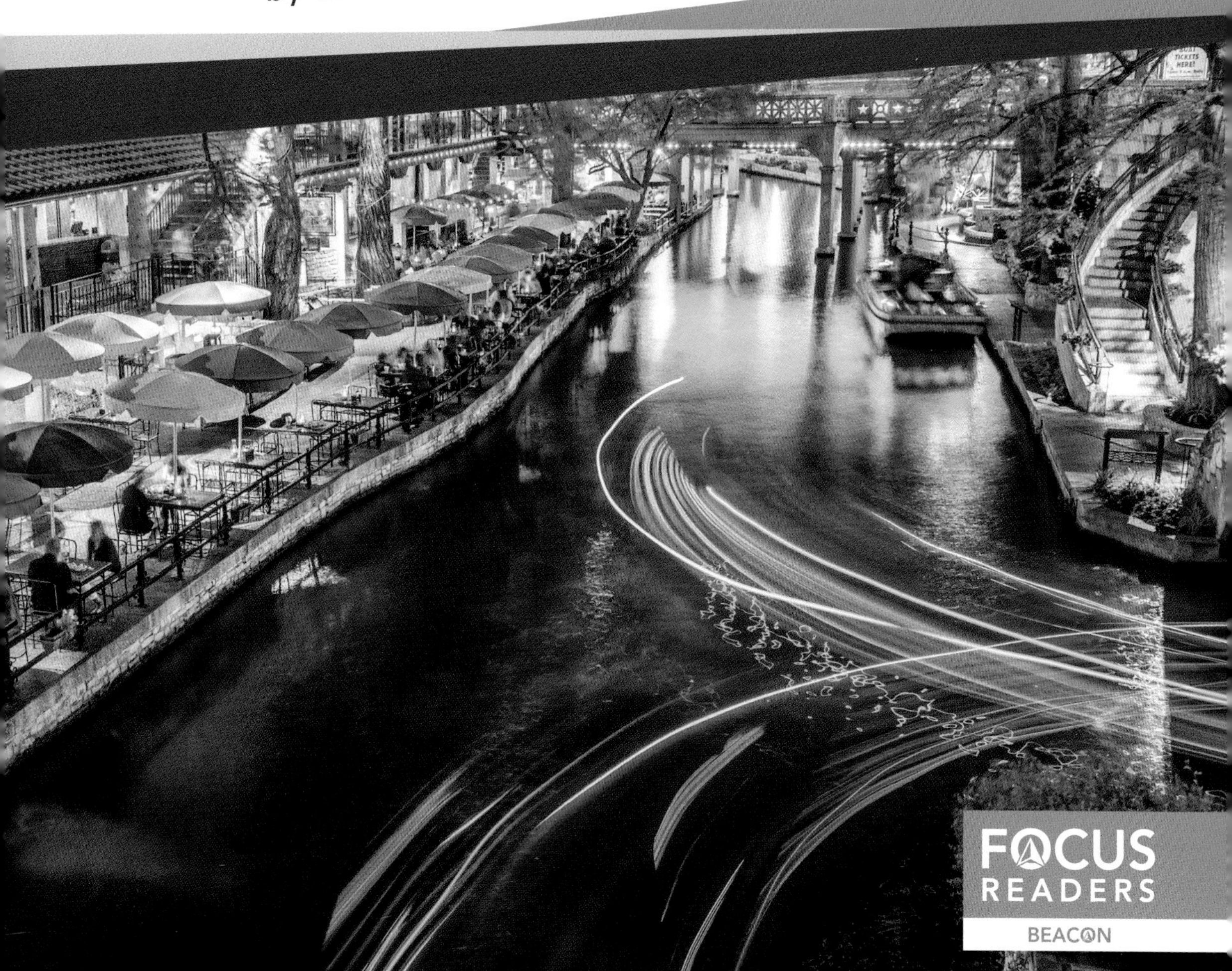

FOCUS READERS

BEACON

www.focusreaders.com

Focus Readers is distributed by North Star Editions:
sales@northstareditions.com | 888-417-0195

Produced for Focus Readers by Red Line Editorial.

Photographs ©: dszc/iStockphoto, cover, 1, 22, 25; James Kirkikis/Shutterstock Images, 4; joshuaraineyphotography/iStockphoto, 7; David Pellerin/Corpus Christi Caller-Times/AP Images, 8; CrackerClips/iStockphoto, 11; f11photo/Shutterstock Images, 13; travelpixpro/iStockphoto, 14, 29; Ceneri/iStockphoto, 17; 400tmax/iStockphoto, 19; Pglam/iStockphoto, 20–21; Red Line Editorial, 27

Library of Congress Cataloging-in-Publication Data
Names: Huddleston, Emma, author.
Title: Exploring the San Antonio River Walk / by Emma Huddleston.
Description: Lake Elmo, MN : Focus Readers, [2020] | Series: Travel America's landmarks | Includes bibliographical references and index. | Audience: Grades 4-6.
Identifiers: LCCN 2019006354 (print) | LCCN 2019021324 (ebook) | ISBN 9781641859899 (pdf) | ISBN 9781641859257 (ebook) | ISBN 9781641857871 (hardcover) | ISBN 9781641858564 (pbk.)
Subjects: LCSH: Paseo del Rio (San Antonio, Tex.)--History--Juvenile literature. | San Antonio (Tex.)--Description and travel--Juvenile literature.
Classification: LCC F394.S2117 (ebook) | LCC F394.S2117 H83 2020 (print) | DDC 917.64/351--dc23
LC record available at https://lccn.loc.gov/2019006354

Printed in the United States of America
Mankato, MN
May, 2019

About the Author

Emma Huddleston lives in the Twin Cities with her husband. She enjoys writing children's books, but she likes reading novels even more. When she is not writing or reading, she likes to stay active by running and swing dancing. She thinks America's landmarks are fascinating and wants to visit them all!

Table of Contents

Chapter 1

Nature in the City

Walkways curve along the San Antonio River. People cross the river on bridges. They wave at the boats floating by. Visitors eat outside at restaurants. They sit under bright umbrellas.

The San Antonio River Walk is a popular place for people to visit.

The San Antonio River Walk joins nature and city life. The walk is often crowded. It is extra busy during **festivals**. People decorate the riverboats. They use red, white, and blue streamers in the summer. They use colorful lights in the winter.

San Antonio has a New Year's celebration. Paper lanterns and flowers float down the river.

The riverboats light up at night.

Every year, millions of people visit San Antonio, Texas. They explore the River Walk. They go shopping. They visit museums. And they learn about San Antonio's history.

Chapter 2

History of the River Walk

In 1921, the San Antonio River flooded. Approximately 9 feet (2.7 m) of water covered a city street. More than 50 people died. Buildings were damaged. People thought the river was dangerous.

Some parts of the San Antonio River are more likely to flood than others.

They added a footbridge. A few shops opened. The city held its first River Walk parade in 1941. A crowd gathered to celebrate.

The River Walk expanded in the 1950s and 1960s. Restaurants, hotels, and shops opened. Workers planted a garden along the river.

The original Olmos Dam had a road across its top. Workers removed the road during a repair in 1981.

Visitors can walk along sidewalks and over bridges to get around the River Walk.

More and more people visited. The River Walk became an exciting destination for visitors.

Chapter 3

Heart of the City

History meets the modern city at the San Antonio River Walk. People can walk from the water to historic sites. These sites include **missions** built in the early 1700s.

Mission Espada is a destination along the River Walk.

At the time, Spain controlled the region. The missions were Spanish communities. People who went to them learned Spanish language and **culture**. Each mission had living spaces, a church, and stone walls.

Four missions still exist near the River Walk. Mission Espada is the oldest. It was founded in 1690 in a town northwest of San Antonio. It moved to San Antonio in 1731. Mission San José is the largest. The church is still active today.

Visitors can attend church services in Mission San José.

The Alamo, a historic **fort**, is also within walking distance of the river. It was the site of a major battle. Texas used to be a part of Mexico. But many people living there wanted to join the United States.

They fought a Mexican army at the Alamo in 1836. The Mexican army won. But Texas later became a US state in 1845.

Visitors learn about the past at the River Walk. But they also visit modern shops. These businesses depend on **tourists** spending money. The money also helps pay

Many tourists come to San Antonio to see the Alamo.

for construction and repair. For example, the city must keep Olmos Dam in good condition. Tourism supports the city of San Antonio.

THAT'S AMAZING!

La Villita

La Villita was a small, Spanish farming town. It is more than 300 years old. Over time, the city of San Antonio was built up around it. In 1939, city officials decided to **restore** La Villita. They made it a center for art and community. They also wanted to recognize its place in history. In 1972, La Villita joined the National Register for Historic Places.

Today, La Villita is a popular place to go on the River Walk. People visit craft and dance events. Shops sell colorful art and homemade jewelry. People enjoy the town's history.

La Villita is a historic neighborhood in San Antonio.

F.W. McALLISTER
Guadalajara Grill
SINCE 1991
OPEN
Shops & Galleries
Restaurants
Arneson River Theatre
GUADALAJARA GRILL
Since 1991
RESTAURANT BAR

Chapter 4

Visiting the River Walk

The San Antonio River Walk is 15 miles (24 km) long. The walk is divided into three main areas. The Downtown Reach is the most popular area. People take riverboat tours. They listen to live music.

The River Walk extends into downtown San Antonio.

They go to shops and restaurants. Crowds gather here for festivals.

The Mission Reach is home to the four missions. It also has 15 miles (24 km) of trails around it. Visitors enjoy hiking and biking.

The Museum Reach was finished in 2009. The Witte Museum teaches

All four missions are National Historic Parks. The government decided they are important reminders of history.

Visitors can ride riverboats through the different sections of the River Walk.

visitors about history. People can see ancient mummies and dinosaur bones. The San Antonio Museum of Art shows paintings, sculptures, and more.

People can also visit the San Antonio Zoo. It is less than 4 miles (6 km) from the River Walk. Giraffes eat lettuce out of people's hands. Butterflies land on people in the butterfly garden.

The River Walk is the heart of San Antonio culture. It gives people a

A canoe race happens on the San Antonio River each year. People come from all over the United States to attend.

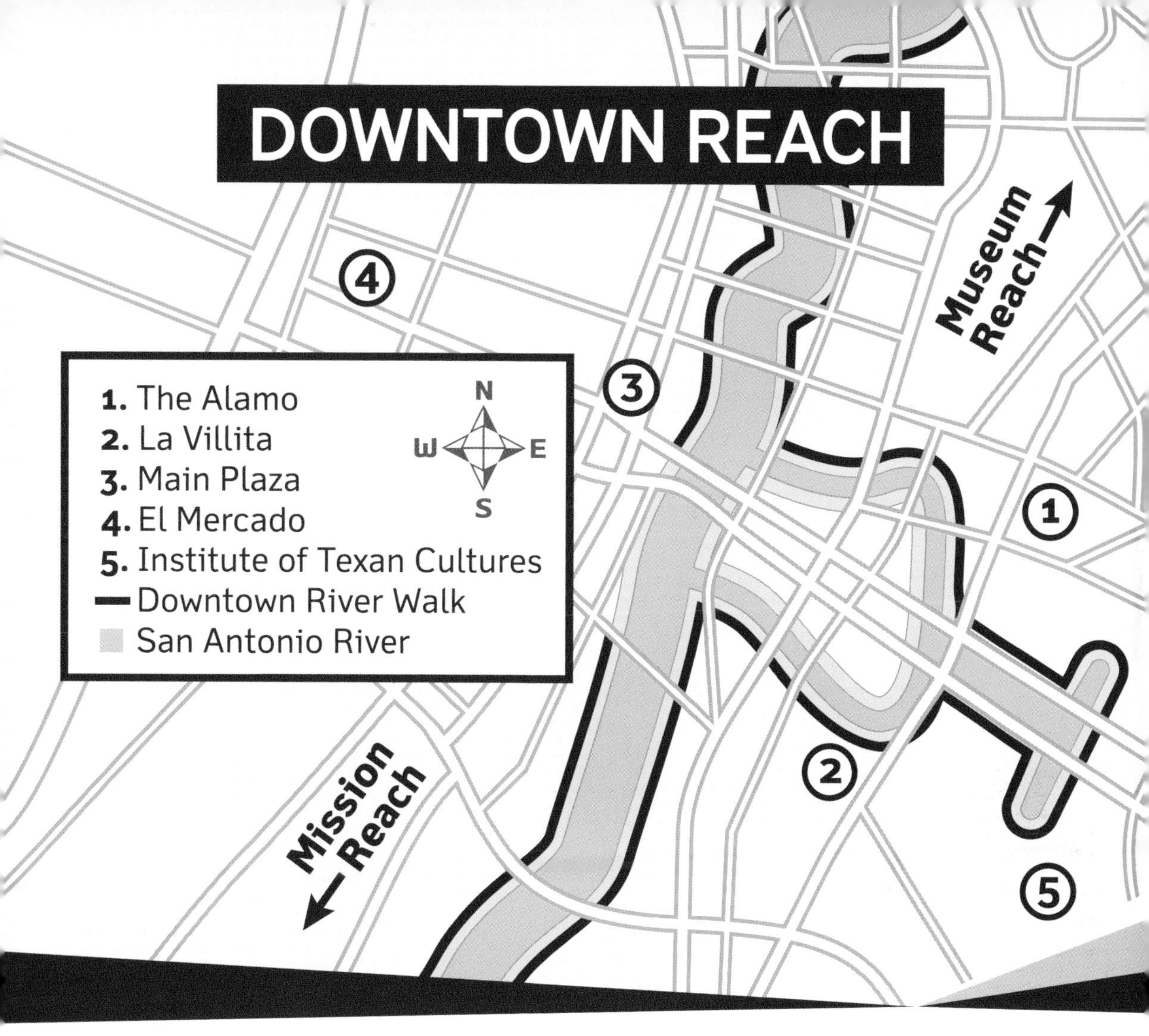

chance to learn about history. It offers modern activities. The River Walk combines nature, the city, and the past.

FOCUS ON THE

San Antonio River Walk

Write your answers on a separate piece of paper.

1. Write a letter to a friend describing the history of the San Antonio River Walk.
2. Which part of the San Antonio River Walk would you want to see first? Why?
3. When was Olmos Dam built?
   A. 1926
   B. 1941
   C. 1939
4. What did city leaders have to do before building the River Walk?
   A. have a festival to tell the city about the River Walk
   B. protect the city from floodwaters
   C. go on a riverboat tour to see the land

5. What does **destination** mean in this book?

*More and more people visited. The River Walk became an exciting **destination** for visitors.*

A. a homeland or place of origin
B. the place where boats enter the water
C. a place that people go to

6. What does **historic** mean in this book?

*They also wanted to recognize its place in history. In 1972, La Villita joined the National Register for **Historic** Places.*

A. new or modern
B. old or forgotten
C. important in history

Answer key on page 32.

Glossary

architect
A person who designs buildings and makes construction plans.

culture
The way a group of people live; their customs, beliefs, and laws.

dam
A wall that stops water from flowing.

festivals
Celebrations that are often held each year in the same place.

fort
A protected building or area of land.

missions
Settlements established by a church to grow its religion.

repair
The action of fixing something.

restore
To return something to its original condition.

sewers
Underground drains for water and waste.

tourists
People who visit an area for fun or enjoyment.

To Learn More

BOOKS

Gagne, Tammy. *Exploring the Southwest.* Minneapolis: Abdo Publishing, 2018.

Lanser, Amanda. *What's Great About Texas?* Minneapolis: Lerner Publications, 2015.

Micklos, John, Jr. *To the Last Man: The Battle of the Alamo.* North Mankato, MN: Capstone Press, 2016.

NOTE TO EDUCATORS

Visit **www.focusreaders.com** to find lesson plans, activities, links, and other resources related to this title.

Index

Answer Key: 1. Answers will vary; **2.** Answers will vary; **3.** A; **4.** B; **5.** C; **6.** C